MOLLY'S SEASONS

DEDICATED
TO NORMAN

MOLLY'S
SEASONS

written and illustrated by
ELLEN KANDOIAN

COBBLEHILL BOOKS
Dutton/New York

Library of Congress Cataloging-in-Publication Data
Kandoian, Ellen.
Molly's seasons / written and illustrated by Ellen Kandoian.
        p.   cm.
Summary: Molly observes the changing seasons in Maine and wonders
what it is like in other parts of the world when the seasons change.
ISBN 0-525-65076-8
1. Seasons—Juvenile literature.   [1. Seasons.]
I. Title.
QB637.4.K36   1992   508—dc20   91-8039   CIP   AC

Published in the United States by
Cobblehill Books,
an affiliate of Dutton Children's Books,
a division of Penguin USA Inc.,
375 Hudson Street, New York, NY 10014

Typography and jacket design by Kathleen Westray
Printed in Hong Kong
First Edition
10 9 8 7 6 5 4 3 2 1

The sun and the snow, the wind and the rain,
Bring signs of the seasons to Molly in Maine.

Fall comes in September when summertime goes—

With apples falling,
Leaves falling,

PICK
YOUR
OWN

Winds swirling,
Squirrels squirreling.

Winter bites in December and chills Molly's toes—

With snow snowing,
Blizzards blowing,

Ice skates gleaming,
Icicles beaming.

When March brings the spring, nearly everything grows—

First, mud flows,
Then grass grows,

And flowers spring,
While birds sing.

Then summertime comes and the evening glows—

With June sun streaming,
Water gleaming,

Berries simmering,
Fireflies glimmering.

But here is what Molly wants to know:
Are the seasons the same wherever you go?

If you travel the whole wide world around,
Will different kinds of seasons be found?

In farthest northern and southern places,

Winter means darkness and noon looks like night,

Summer means sunshine and midnight is bright.

Near the Equator,

As the months of the tropical year go by,
There are two kinds of seasons—rainy

and dry.

In the Southern Hemisphere,

When Molly's summer's just begun,
The tilt of the Earth, with the top toward the sun,
Makes the southern Earth tilt away,
Bringing chilly weather New Zealand's way.

So in New Zealand a boy named Ollie
Has seasons quite a bit like Molly.

But it's winter in June, summer in December,
Autumn in March, and spring in September!

ABOUT THE SEASONS

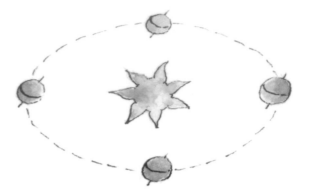

THE SEASONS change because of the changing relationship of the Earth to the sun. The Earth is like a big spinning ball, and the sun is a bright light far away in space. A day passes each time the Earth spins once. A year passes each time the spinning Earth makes one big circle around the sun.

The sun's energy is so powerful that it makes the Earth light and warm, even though the sun is very far away. Whichever part of the Earth is nearest to the sun receives the most light and warmth.

The seasons change during the year as the Earth circles around the sun, like a spinning top, tilted to one side. The upper part of the Earth leans toward the sun part of the year and away part of the year. When the upper part—the Northern Hemisphere—tilts toward the sun, the lower part—the Southern Hemisphere—tilts away.

When the Northern Hemisphere, where Molly lives, tilts toward the sun, it is summer for Molly. She has warmer weather and more hours of daylight. Meanwhile, Ollie in the Southern Hemisphere is having winter.

When the Northern Hemisphere tilts away from the sun, it is winter for Molly. She has colder weather and fewer hours of light. Meanwhile, Ollie in the Southern Hemisphere is having summer.

Near the Equator, an imaginary line that goes around the middle of the Earth, the temperature stays more constant. Changes in the Earth's atmosphere cause seasons of raininess and dryness.

The energy from the sun makes the seasons change, the ice melt, the flowers grow, and the apples ripen. The changing seasons bring children out to play in the warm sun in summer and send them deep under their covers on cold winter nights. The signs of the seasons help us to mark the passing years.